Books by Nancy Luenn
*Arctic Unicorn*
*Unicorn Crossing*

# UNICORN
# CROSSING

Nancy Luenn

# UNICORN CROSSING

*illustrated by*
*Peter E. Hanson*

Atheneum • New York • 1987

Text copyright © 1987 by Nancy Luenn
Illustrations copyright © 1987 by Peter E. Hanson

Atheneum
Macmillan Publishing Company
866 Third Avenue, New York, NY 10022
Collier Macmillan Canada, Inc.

Type set by V & M Graphics, New York City
Printed and bound by Fairfield Graphics, Fairfield, Pennsylvania
Designed by Mary Ahern
Calligraphy by Jeanyee Wong
First Edition

10    9    8    7    6    5    4    3    2    1

Library of Congress Cataloging–in–Publication Data

Luenn, Nancy.    Unicorn crossing.

SUMMARY: Jenny hopes to fulfill her desire to see
a real unicorn on her vacation when she helps old Mrs. Donovan
pick roses one misty morning.
[1. Unicorns—Fiction] I. Hanson, Peter E., ill. II. Title.
PZ7.L9766Un    1987    [Fic]    87–995
ISBN 0-689-31384-5

*For Rick, who, like Jenny,*
*has his own individual vision*
*and for John and Margaret,*
*who invited me to Unicorn Crossing*

# CONTENTS

# UNICORN
# CROSSING

# ONE

# The Sign in the Woods

Jenny stood on the deck of the ferry, watching the island grow bigger. Dark green trees cloaked the low hills. It looked like a place that kept secrets.

There are places no one has ever discovered, she thought. Caves and hidden pools, and clearings that turn silver in the moonlight.

"Maybe unicorns live there," she said aloud.

"Don't be dumb," said her older sister, Monica. "Unicorns aren't real."

They *are* real, thought Jenny. I almost saw one on my last birthday. I just have to find the right place.

She leaned against the rail and wondered what was hidden by the trees. There might be a unicorn drinking from a pool somewhere deep in that forest. She closed her eyes. The unicorn's tail was trailing in the water. He raised his head. Light from his horn sparkled in ripples. . . .

The ferry whistle boomed overhead. Startled, Jenny clutched the railing and opened her eyes. She saw cormorants and gulls perched on wooden pilings. As the ferry nudged its way toward the dock, the pilings creaked softly.

"Race you to the car!" shouted Monica. Jenny scrambled down the stairs in pursuit, but she knew Monica would win.

The air inside the car was warm and still. Ahead of them, cars rumbled off the ferry two by two.

"Mrs. Donovan lives in the main house," her dad said, as he started the engine. "We'll be staying in her cottage." The ramp clattered as they drove onto the dock.

"Will we *really* be near the beach?" Monica asked again.

"Yes," said her dad patiently.

"And there's a rowboat!" added her mom. Jenny sighed. Her mom wanted to take them fishing and horseback riding and digging for clams.

I'd rather look for unicorns, she thought.

They drove down the main street of town, and turned onto a side road. After passing a few blocks of quiet old houses, the road hurried into the country. Farmhouses nestled in their fields, watching over orchards and grazing cows. Soon, tall trees leaned above the road. Jenny looked out the open window. Outside the car it was green and quiet.

It smells right, she thought, taking a deep breath. It smells like cool cinnamon. She searched among the trees for signs of unicorns.

They drove out of the forest suddenly, and swooped along the shore. Across still blue water, she saw the tall towers of a distant kingdom. Polished stones sparkled in the sunlight. Turrets sprang up to touch the sky.

"Look!" shouted Monica, squeezing against Jenny. "There's the Space Needle." The kingdom crumbled, leaving behind the hazy city skyscrapers of Seattle.

"Stop pushing, Monica!" said Jenny.

"No fighting, girls," her mom said. "We're almost there."

They drove up a hill and away from the water. Trees drew closer to the road. Jenny watched light creep into the woods and dance on patches of bright grass. Then she saw a sudden flash of white through the dark trees. She leaned

further out the window. There it was again!

A long tail swished as something stirred in the shadows. Jenny held her breath. Her heart began to pound. Something moved gracefully through the forest, half-hidden by the trees. Sunbeams gleamed on white flanks and a flowing mane. The unicorn stepped into the sunlight.

"Look, Jenny!" said Monica. "A horse!"

"I saw it," mumbled Jenny. It *was* only a horse, with big heavy hooves. She looked away.

The car slowed to turn onto a dirt driveway. There was a round white sign caught in the bushes. Her heart started pounding again. The sign said "Unicorn Crossing."

# TWO

# *A Perfect Place for Unicorns*

The sign was like a circle of lace in the leafy green woods. A unicorn was carved above the words "Unicorn Crossing."

This is it! thought Jenny. This must be the place. She leaned across to look out Monica's window.

"Move over," demanded Monica. Jenny looked out the rear window instead. The sign had vanished in the trees.

"When can I go riding?" asked Monica, as the car bumped up the drive.

"Tomorrow," said her mother. "You and me and Jenny."

Jenny sank down on the seat. She wanted to look for unicorns. Ahead of them, the trees gave way to brilliant green lawn and sunshine. Cow parsnips grew as high as the eaves of Mrs. Donovan's house. The car stopped, and she scrambled out behind Monica.

"Wow!" said Monica. Jenny was silent, but for once she agreed with her sister.

She saw a tall white arch covered with roses. Vines of roses climbed along the fence and over a trellis above the porch. Mrs. Donovan's house was wonderful, too. It stretched out along the porch like a cat in the sun. There were dozens and dozens of small glass panes in the windows and doors. The low brown roof was capped by three brick chimneys.

It's like a place in a story! thought

Jenny, smiling at the bright blue porch and open doors. She took a deep breath. The air smelled of saltwater and roses.

There was an empty birdbath on the lawn. Flowers hid the path that led to the archway. Beyond it, a meadow sloped down to the water. An immense mountain floated in the distance, crowned with a cap of clouds.

"Look at Mt. Rainier!" her dad said.

"What a great place to ride!" added her mom.

"Yippee!" shouted Monica. She dashed across the lawn, climbed the gate and raced toward the water.

"Monica!" shouted her dad, but Monica didn't stop.

"She'll be fine," said a soft, old voice. Jenny turned and saw an elderly woman standing on the porch. She walked under the roses and came to greet them.

"I'm Mrs. Donovan."

Mrs. Donovan's white hair was coiled in braids around her head. Her face was wrinkled, but her eyes looked young. She wore a Japanese kimono covered with flowers, and red slippers with long curling toes.

"Hello, Jenny," she said. She didn't pinch Jenny's cheek or pat her on the head.

"Hello," Jenny whispered, surprised that Mrs. Donovan knew her name. She gave Mrs. Donovan a shy smile.

She followed the grownups under the trellis of roses onto the porch. The porch was so blue it was like walking on the sky.

I wonder if Mrs. Donovan has ever seen a unicorn? Jenny thought. She imagined her standing on the lawn in her red kimono, pouring water from a silver pitcher into the birdbath. When it was full, a unicorn would come quietly out of the woods to drink....

"Come on, Jenny," called her mom impatiently. They went down the steps and she saw a worn brick path leading to a curved gate in the archway. It's perfect, she thought, the unicorn could come right through that gate. Reluctantly, she turned and followed the grownups around a corner of the lawn. There was the cottage, tucked in behind the main house. Mrs. Donovan opened the door.

"I picked you a bowl of strawberries this morning," the old woman said. "There are towels on the counter and the sheets are fresh." The cottage smelled of pine cleanser. Jenny's image of the unicorn and Mrs. Donovan began to fade.

No, she thought. Grownups don't believe in unicorns.

# THREE

# *Mrs. Donovan*

In the morning, Jenny slipped outside while the others were still eating breakfast. As she closed the door, she could hear Monica talking loudly about horses.

Maybe I'll have time to explore, she thought. Between the walls of Mrs. Donovan's house and the cottage was a pathway leading to a tall wooden fence. The gate was open. Jenny climbed the steps and went quietly through the gate.

Grapevines made a cool green roof above her head. A fountain splashed in the middle of a formal garden. Box hedges marched along the path leading to the fountain. Jenny let out her breath in a delighted sigh.

An enchanted garden! she thought. The air was warm and peaceful. Jenny started down the flagstone path toward the fountain. Birds sang undisturbed in the trees overhead. Bees hummed and the fountain chuckled, juggling rainbows in the sun.

Jenny tiptoed forward and rested her elbows on the stone rim of the pool. Goldfish darted beneath the falling water. She looked up through the spray of the fountain. Hidden in the thicket sheltering the garden was another tall white archway. She squeezed through the hedge and walked toward it.

The statue of a smiling woman stood in green shadows under the arch. She wore a long red robe of painted stone. A wreath of berries crowned her head, and she cradled a basket of fruit and grain. Jenny looked thoughtfully at the woman's face.

"She looks like a queen," she said aloud.

"She is a queen," an old voice replied, "the queen of summer."

Jenny spun around, her heart pounding. Mrs. Donovan was kneeling behind a hedge, pulling weeds. Her white hair was covered by a battered green hat.

"Oh," said Jenny. She took a step backwards. Mrs. Donovan sat back on her heels and smiled.

"Welcome to my garden," she said. She bent her head and began weeding again.

Jenny sat on the rim of the fountain and watched Mrs. Donovan pulling weeds. After a while, the old woman stood up slowly, brushing dirt from her knees and hands. She set her trowel on the low stone wall.

"Come and see my house," she suggested.

Mrs. Donovan walked under the grapevine trellis and opened a back door to her house. Jenny followed her into a hallway of soft colors and old photographs. At the end of the hall, another door opened into the living room.

Jenny stopped in the middle of the room. Light spilled over the jade green walls. A low green bench stood on the hearth and trailing flowers brightened the fireplace. She stared at the painting hanging above the mantel. A shaggy unicorn reared against the moon. Snow flew from his hooves and his breath drifted in clouds.

"Do you like unicorns?" she asked shyly.

"Very much," replied Mrs. Donovan. "Would you like to see *my* unicorns?"

# FOUR

# What Do Unicorns Eat?

Mrs. Donovan led her through a dim bedroom into a room of many windows. Bookshelves lined the walls beneath them. Instead of holding books, the shelves were filled with unicorns.

"Oh!" said Jenny. "They're wonderful!" She knelt on the pale blue rug and looked at them one by one.

There was a tiny spun glass unicorn the color of the sea. An ivory unicorn knelt beside a Chinese unicorn of jade. She ran one finger along a wooden unicorn's smooth flanks. There were unicorns made of china, cut from paper,

and chiseled from stone. She picked up a patchwork velvet unicorn and turned to smile at Mrs. Donovan.

Above the old woman's chair hung a photograph. Jenny stopped smiling and stared at the picture on the wall.

The photograph was faded and a

little out of focus. But Jenny could see a delicate white face and a cloud of mane. A white forelock cascaded between alert ears, and above the ears . . .

Jenny blinked and looked again. Above the ears was a thin, pointed shadow.

No, not a shadow. A horn!

"Can you see it, Jenny?" asked Mrs. Donovan.

"It's a unicorn!"

Mrs. Donovan laughed softly. "Most people can't see the horn. I tell them he was a pony I had as a little girl. He came into our garden to eat."

"What do unicorns eat?" Jenny asked, excitement bubbling inside her. She leaned forward.

"Roses," Mrs. Donovan whispered. "Just the petals."

Jenny remembered the rose vines on the fence outside.

"Here?" she squeaked. Mrs. Donovan didn't seem to hear her question.

"I used to pick rose petals for him," she said. "I had to be very quiet."

Jenny hugged the patchwork unicorn a little tighter. "If there were unicorns here," she said slowly, "would I see them?"

Mrs. Donovan smiled. "I think so."

"What about Monica?" she asked. "Would she see them?"

"She's too old for unicorns," said Mrs. Donovan. "You have to be just the right age."

"Am I the right age?" asked Jenny anxiously.

"Yes," the old woman said, "and so am I."

Jenny puzzled over this. Mrs. Donovan was a lot older than Monica. It didn't make sense. Just then she heard her mom calling.

"Jenny! We're ready to go." Her mom sounded annoyed.

Jenny put down the patchwork unicorn reluctantly. "I have to leave," she said, and hurried into the hall. She heard Monica's voice and the crunch of gravel on the path outside.

"Jenny, where are you? Let's go!"

# FIVE

# Unicorn in the Forest

Jenny perched nervously on the broad back of a pony. The brown pony plodded across the meadow behind her mom's horse. Monica on hers, galloped past them.

"Isn't this great?" she shouted.

No, thought Jenny. She wanted to get down, but the ground seemed too far away. She clung to the saddle and thought about unicorns.

If there are unicorns here, she wondered, where would they be? Her pony suddenly decided to trot. She clutched the saddlehorn and held on tight.

"He can smell the stables," said her mom. "Pull in the reins, honey." She slowed her horse to walk beside Jenny's pony. When they reached the stables, Jenny slid gratefully out of the saddle.

"Can I come again tomorrow?" Monica asked.

"Of course," said her mom. "What about you, Jenny?" She shook her head, trying not to mind her mother's frown.

Tomorrow, she thought, I'm going to look for unicorns.

The next day she walked down the brick path and opened the curved white gate. Closing it carefully behind her, she started down the hill. At the bottom of the hill was a green pond surrounded by willows. Jenny skirted the willows and climbed up into the forest. It was quiet under the huge trees. She stopped to catch her breath, then walked deeper into the woods.

If there are unicorns here, she thought, this is where they would be. Moss-covered maples stood among the towering firs. Graceful elderberries grew out of fallen logs and tiny white flowers sprinkled the ground.

Jenny sat down under a solemn old maple tree. Around her, ferns sprang out of matted needles on the forest floor. She imagined she was a princess waiting for a unicorn. She smoothed out an invisible velvet skirt and waited patiently. Above the silence she began to hear small noises. A woodpecker drummed in the distance, and further off she heard the cries of gulls.

After a while, a squirrel skittered down a tree trunk. He sat up to look at her, then whisked away. A deeper hush fell over the forest. She gazed at bright green leaves and deep green shadows. Sunlight turned the brown trunks golden. The whole forest held its breath.

The unicorn came slowly toward her through the trees. A ray of light reflected from his forehead as he melted into the shadows. His tiny hooves made no sound. She glimpsed a mane as fine as a cloud of downy white feathers. Slowly, he stepped out of the shadows. A stick cracked beneath one hoof. Jenny blinked.

"Hi, Jenny!" said Monica. She was sitting on a fat white pony. "Don't you want to come riding?"

Jenny shook her head. Her eyes felt hot. She was afraid she would cry if she said anything.

It's just a dumb pony, she thought. She watched Monica slap the reins and urge him into a trot. Sticks crackled under his hooves as her sister rode off through the forest.

Jenny shifted uncomfortably. The ground beneath her was damp and prickly. An ant crawled across her hand.

She shook it off and stood up.

Monica spoiled it, she thought. I'll get up tomorrow while she's still asleep. Maybe then I'll see a unicorn.

# SIX

# Unicorn
# in the Fog

When Jenny woke up the next morning, Monica was tugging at her sleeve.

"Wake up! Dad's going to take us to the tidepools."

Jenny sighed as she climbed out of bed. Maybe tomorrow I'll be the first one up, she thought. But on the following day her mom woke them both up early to go fishing.

When Jenny opened her eyes on the third morning, she sat up cautiously. Monica was still asleep. She listened for a moment. It was quiet in the cottage. She pulled on her clothes and tiptoed outside.

It was very foggy. She could faintly see the roses on the fence, but everything beyond the arch was cloaked in gray. She went silently across the lawn and slipped through the gate. As she walked down the hill, wet grass soaked the legs of her jeans. She heard the booming horn of a ferry in the distance.

When she reached the meadow, she could hear the waves lapping the shore, but she couldn't see the water. She could see the grass under her feet, but everything else was invisible. Dampness clung to her skin. She shivered and put her hands in her pockets.

Jenny planted her feet on the firm ground and watched the fog drift across the meadow. The dark green spire of a tree appeared, then was swallowed by the mist.

Maybe it will swallow me, too, she thought uneasily. She turned in a slow circle. When the fog lifted would everything have changed? Maybe she would be in a different world. Jenny stopped. Her heart began to pound.

A ghostly shape raced toward her through the fog. Its mane and tail streamed into the mist, fading into gray. It skimmed the ground, silent, swift as dreams. Clouds tattered on its horn. The unicorn came flying toward her, snow white in the summer mist.

"Raven! White Raven!" A woman's clear voice cut through the fog. The unicorn stopped and looked at her sideways.

Jenny bit her lip. It was a dog. The most beautiful dog she had ever seen, with tasseled ears and huge brown eyes, but still, it was only a dog.

She hunched her shoulders and jammed her hands against the bottom of her pockets. Behind the white dog, a woman was striding through the mist. She wore a deep red robe and a wreath of berries.

It's the summer queen! thought Jenny. The one from the garden! As she drew near, Jenny stared at her flowing red robe. There was something odd about it.

Buttons, she thought miserably. It has buttons. It's a raincoat. She looked at the wreath and saw that the leaves and berries were a woven design on a red and green scarf. Jenny began to shiver. Her shoes were soaking wet and her jeans felt clammy.

"Hello," said the woman. "You look cold." She took off her scarf and bent down beside Jenny. "Here." She wrapped the scarf around Jenny's head and smiled. "You must be Monica or Jenny." Her hazel eyes were gentle and a little sad. She looked like someone who is good at listening.

"I'm Jenny."

"And I'm Mary Morgan. I live up the hill from Mrs. Donovan. Let's get you home right away."

They followed the dog through the long wet grass. His plumed tail waved gently as he led the way.

"What kind of dog is that?" asked Jenny.

"Raven is a saluki," the woman said, "an Arabian greyhound."

"I thought he was a unicorn," said Jenny wistfully.

Mary Morgan laughed softly. "I used to think there were unicorns here," she said. "But I never saw one." Her voice was sad. She stopped outside Mrs. Donovan's gate.

"Don't look too hard," she said as she opened the gate. "That's what Mrs. Donovan used to tell me." She gave Jenny another smile and whistled to her dog.

Jenny watched her climb over the wooden stile and start across the next field. White Raven was racing back and forth, in and out of the fog. He looked like a unicorn again. Mary Morgan was as tall and graceful as a queen.

But she's not, thought Jenny. She tugged at the red and green scarf. It's just Mary Morgan and her dog. Her teeth chattered. She closed the gate and ran toward the cottage.

# SEVEN

# Maybe Unicorns Aren't Real

For the rest of the week, Jenny didn't look for unicorns. She helped Mrs. Donovan pull weeds in her garden. She walked on the beach with Mary Morgan and her dog. She even went riding again with her mom and Monica.

On Saturday, Jenny and her dad drove into town and bought groceries at the store. On the way back, she saw a flash of white in the woods near Mary Morgan's house.

It's only White Raven, she thought, and sighed.

"What's wrong, Jenny?" asked her dad. He slowed the car to turn into Mrs. Donovan's driveway. She could feel him waiting patiently for her reply.

"I was hoping for a unicorn," she said.

"Oh, Jenny," he said gently, "there aren't any unicorns here on the island."

She put her chin on her hands and stared at the Unicorn Crossing sign. "Then why does Mrs. Donovan have that sign?" she asked. "And why is her house called Unicorn Crossing?"

"Well," her dad said, "because she likes unicorns, I suppose. The same way I like griffins. Lots of people like imaginary animals." Jenny stared out the window at the cow parsnips.

"But a long time ago," she said, "unicorns were real."

"That's possible," said her dad, as he parked on the grass. "They could be extinct, like dinosaurs."

Jenny slowly unbuckled her seat belt. She placed one hand on the door handle. Extinct. Gone. No more unicorns.

Maybe Monica is right, she thought sadly. Mary Morgan had looked, and she never saw one.

Jenny got out of the car. She carried

a bag of groceries along the blue porch toward the cottage. The roses on the fence and archway glowed in the sunlight like deep red velvet. Jenny set the groceries on the porch railing and stared at them.

Roses are real, she thought. Mrs. Donovan says unicorns eat roses. How can something that isn't real eat something that is?

# EIGHT

# The Open Gate

Jenny woke at dawn. Someone had called her name very softly. She pulled on her clothes and tiptoed outside. Mrs. Donovan was waiting in the gray morning light, dressed in her silk kimono. She carried a big empty basket.

"Come and help me pick roses," whispered the old woman. Jenny nodded, unable to say a word.

Roses! she thought. Suddenly she felt hopeful again.

She followed Mrs. Donovan down the steps of the cottage. A nighttime quiet lingered in the air. Even the birdsongs overhead seemed muted. They walked across the lawn, leaving wet footprints in the grass.

When they reached the fence, Mrs. Donovan set down the wicker basket. She began pulling petals off the roses that grew on top of the fence. Jenny reached for the ones lower down. The roses were the color of Mary Morgan's coat. Dew nestled in their golden hearts and the petals were silky smooth. She rubbed one against her cheek before dropping it into the basket.

Will the unicorn really come? she wondered. She listened carefully, but all she could hear were birds singing and a squirrel rustling the leaves.

As she picked the petals, thorns scratched at her fingers. She chewed her lip and glanced up. There were red streaks on Mrs. Donovan's old hands. She looked down at her own. They were all covered with scratches.

These are for the unicorn, she thought, reaching for another flower. Her scratches stung.

But what if unicorns aren't real? The question buzzed around her like a wasp. It was even harder to ignore than her stinging hands. But she pushed it away and tugged the petals from another rose. After a while she looked down at the basket. It was only half full.

What if Monica wakes up before we finish? she worried. She tried picking petals faster, but the thorns caught her fingers. Overhead she heard the harsh laughter of a crow.

Maybe it's just a game, thought Jenny. She stopped and looked up at Mrs. Donovan. The old woman was smiling as she picked the deep red petals. She hummed softly and her cheeks were very pink. As Jenny watched, she shook a vine, and a shower of dew fell shining on her braided white hair. Mrs. Donovan's smile deepened.

Mrs. Donovan believes in unicorns, decided Jenny, or she wouldn't be so happy. She took a deep breath. The cool scent of roses spilled over her. She reached out and pulled the petals from another rose.

At last the basket was full. Mrs. Donovan carried it across the lawn, emptied it into the dry birdbath, and opened the white gate. Then she turned and walked back up the brick path.

Jenny stood beside her near the porch steps, staring through the open gate. The willows by the pond seemed to shimmer in the morning mist. Behind them stood the dark fir forest, mysterious and silent. If I look in just the right place, she thought, and in just the right way . . .

"Don't look too hard," Mrs. Donovan said softly.

Jenny blinked. She heard a whisper of sound beyond the gate.

# NINE

# Roses in the Birdbath

Brightness filled the air outside the gate. A unicorn bent its neck and stepped under the arch. Another followed, and another. She caught her breath as each slender horn cleared the tangle of roses. They were the size of ponies, but looked as if they could fly.

The unicorns pranced on shining cloven hooves toward the birdbath. Their horns glowed like wax candles. They lowered their heads and began to eat without making a sound.

Jenny gazed at the unicorns, forgetting to breathe, then gasping each time

she remembered. They were like new snow, and kittens, and the moon.

I wonder how they can stand so close together, she thought. Their ivory horns crossed without ever touching, but their manes and tails flowed around them like clouds. From time to time, one of them stamped a silent bright hoof on the grass.

They're eating the rose petals I picked, thought Jenny proudly. Now she didn't mind the scratches. She stood very still and watched the unicorns eating from the birdbath.

When the air turned gold with sunrise, the unicorns raised their heads and drifted lightly toward the gate. Their horns became brighter and brighter as the sun came up behind the forest. They shone so brightly that Jenny closed her eyes. She opened them a single breath later, but the unicorns were gone. Outside the gate, a feathery white mist lingered in the morning light. She turned in a slow circle, wondering if she had really seen them. Then she stopped and stared. The birdbath on the lawn was empty, and the air smelled of cinnamon and roses.